my Cat

A SCRAPBOOK OF DRAWINGS, PHOTOS, AND FACTS

BY MARILYN BAILLIE

ILLUSTRATED BY BRENDA CLARK

LITTLE, BROWN AND COMPANY

BOSTON NEW YORK TORONTO LONDON

For Charles, Matthew, Jonathan and Alexandra — *M.B.*

For Aaron and Soupy — *B.C.*

All about my cat

This book is all about your cat, that extra-special furry friend. There are spaces for you to write down your cat's funny habits, and places for pictures of your cat. You'll also discover amazing cat facts and find out how to make great cat toys and treats.

So get started by drawing a picture or attaching a photo of your cat in the picture frame here. Then grab a pencil or pen and fill in the information below.

My cat

My cat's name is _____.

Nicknames I call my cat are _____, _____, _____.

My cat is ☐ a kitten ☐ an adult cat

My cat is ☐ male ☐ female

My cat is about _____ years, _____ months old.

My cat is as big as a _____.

The date I got my cat was _____.

The first thing my cat did when we arrived home was _____

_____.

One incredible

What color is your cat? How long is her tail? Check off the boxes here to describe what your cat looks like. There's even a place for you to draw in all her spots, stripes, and markings. What are you waiting for?

My cat's eyes are:

☐ blue ☐ green ☐ yellow ☐ other

My cat's ears are:

☐ tall and pointed ☐ medium ☐ small and pointed ☐ other

My cat's color is:

☐ black ☐ white ☐ brown ☐ calico ☐ orange ☐ othe

My cat's fur is:

☐ long and fluffy ☐ sleek and short ☐ other

My cat has these special markings:

cat!

My cat's whiskers are:

☐ short

☐ long

☐ really long

My cat's tail is:

☐ as long as my hand

☐ as long as my whole arm

☐ as long as my arm from my wrist to my elbow

☐ different from all these

_____

_____

_____

Weigh your cat

It's weigh-in time, and your cat won't stay on the scales. How can you find out how much she weighs?

1. Step on the scales yourself, and remember your weight.

2. Gently pick up your cat and stand on the scales together.

3. Subtract your weight from the weight of the two of you. Now you know how heavy your cat is.

My cat weighs _____ .

A day in the life of _____

(Fill in your cat's name here)

Cats don't pass their time in a ho-hum way, day after day. Many things happen — but you have to watch carefully. Observe your cat for part of a day and make notes, draw pictures, or even take photos to find out just what goes on. Scientists who study animal behavior do the same things when they are trying to learn how animals act.

Put a drawing or photo of your cat in each of the frames here. Then draw in the hands on the clocks to tell when he did what you've shown. Beside each picture, write about what your pet is doing.

Be a cat detective

Be on the lookout for every move or expression your cat makes.

If your cat is sleeping, note where his tail, head, and paws are. Does he always sleep in the same position? Where does he sleep?

When your cat is playing, does he usually choose the same playthings or does he like new toys? Ask yourself as many questions as you can think of, and have fun being a cat detective!

My cat playing

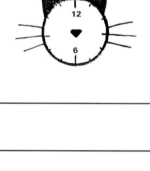

_____
_____
_____
_____

Digging into dinner

_____
_____
_____
_____

Super snoozers

Don't be concerned if your cat seems to snooze a lot. Most cats sleep two-thirds of their time, about twice as much as you do. They take short catnaps, sometimes with their eyes slightly open.

_____

_____

_____

_____

_____

_____

_____

_____

_____

_____

My cat taking a catnap

Groom and stretch time

My cat having fun indoors

I found out _____ new things about my cat today.

I was surprised that my cat

_____

_____ .

My cat

☐ wondered why

☐ didn't realize

I was watching him.

An inside adventure

Find out more about your cat's everyday play habits by trying this:

In a familiar place, put out a large, open, empty paper bag. A paper grocery bag is a good size. Attract your cat to the bag by crinkling the paper. Observe how he approaches it and what he does with it. Take a photo or draw a picture of your cat playing and add it to this page or to the pocket at the back of the book.

Countless cats

Cats come in countless numbers and countless color variations. They can be divided into two big groups according to their coats. Cats can be either shorthaired or longhaired. Within these two groups, there are many breeds of cat, some of which are pictured below. There are also cats that are a mixture of breeds. Is your cat here? If you are not sure if your cat is shorthaired or longhaired or what breed of cat you have, ask your vet next time you go for a visit.

Shorthairs

American shorthair

American shorthairs are descended from hardy street cats. Their bodies are muscular, and their coats come in many different colors. They are excellent mousers and good family pets.

Manx

Manx cats have no tails at all. These unusual cats were first bred on an island off the coast of England.

Burmese

Burmese have sweet faces and are full of mischief. They have been known to open refrigerator doors and get into cupboards when you least expect it!

Siamese

Siamese might not welcome other cats in their house. They love their owners' attention and are loyal pets. They are intelligent, noisy, and talkative.

Sphynx

Since the sphynx has almost no hair, it's a good pet for many people who love cats but are allergic to them. However, although most people are allergic to cat fur and dander, some are allergic to cat saliva. The sphynx doesn't have a furry coat, but it still licks itself like any other cat, so some people are allergic to it.

My cat is shown here and is called a

_____.

My cat is shorthaired and is not here but is called

_____.

I don't know what my cat is, but my cat has short hair and looks like a

_____

Longhairs

Persian

Persians are called the ultimate house cats. Not only are they beautiful, with their long, flowing, woolly coats, but they are also gentle companions.

Birman

Birman cats, it is said, were sacred in temples at one time. They have big blue eyes and their paws are always white.

Scottish fold longhair

These cats are named for their folded ears. Folds are also known for their sad faces. They get on well with people and pets.

Maine coon

The oldest American breed of cat is the Maine coon. These large cats have long coats that thin out in warm weather. Their tails are bushy with rings, a bit like a raccoon's!

My cat is shown here and is called a
_____.

My cat is longhaired and is not here but is called
_____.

I don't know what my cat is, but my cat has long hair and looks like a
_____.

Mixed-breed cats

Mixed-breed cats come from a mixture of two or more breeds. If you are not sure what kind of cat yours is, you may have a mixed breed, either shorthaired or longhaired. Most house cats are mixed breeds, with traits from a wide variety of cats. Some people say that their cats are stronger and healthier that way — they are a superior mix!

My cat is a mixed breed and has a
_____
colored coat.

If I had to guess the mixture of my cat, I'd say my cat is part
_____
and part
_____.

Big cats

Your pet is closely related to some of the most magnificent animals in the world. Lions, tigers, jaguars, cheetahs, as well as other wild cats share many habits and characteristics with your cat. They are all agile, can sprint, jump, and pounce. Grooming keeps them clean and in touch with other cats, and catnaps take up a good part of their time. The big cats probably even look like your cat, with their sleek bodies, soft fur, bristly whiskers, and sharp teeth.

Test how well you know your cat's relatives. Read the clues, then try to identify each of these big cats. The answers are in the bottom right corner.

1.

I am the only cat who lives in a family group, or pride. My mane makes me look large and fierce and I am sometimes called "king." The females in our family do most of the hunting. They share the care of the young and look after the pride. We make our home in Africa.

I am a _____.

My cat ☐ likes to climb trees like a jaguar

☐ never climbs trees

2.

I am the fastest land animal in the world. Since I hunt on the wide-open plains of Africa, I need speed to catch my prey. From a standing start, I can spurt ahead as fast as a racing car. My amazing speed lasts for short distances, but by the time I tire I usually have my meal.

I am a _____.

My cat ☐ likes to swim in water like a tiger

☐ hates swimming

Thunder sounds

"R-o-a-r!" The voice of the lion booms across the African plains. Other large cats such as tigers, jaguars, and leopards roar, too. All members of the cat family communicate with various voices and sounds. Your cat probably meows, gurgles, and purrs, but only the biggest cats can r-o-a-r!

3.

Count me in as the biggest and strongest of the big cats. I live in parts of Asia and India and roam alone over my territory. I prowl through the dense forests or swim in the cool river in search of prey. My stripes keep me hidden until I am ready to attack with my claws and fangs.

I am a _____.

My cat ☐ likes being in a group like a lion

☐ likes to be alone

4.

I am the only large cat that lives in North, South, and Central America. I climb trees and swim rivers to hunt for food. People have taken over my jungle territory and try to catch me for my beautiful coat. But my spots and dots hide me in the trees and bushes.

I am a _____.

My cat ☐ has a very long tail like a cheetah

☐ has a short tail

Answers: 1. lion 2. cheetah 3. tiger 4. jaguar

Cat care and comfort

W hen your cat gives you that "I need something" look, she is also saying "I depend on you."

Stroke her softly and give her a hug. Then, think of what she might be trying to tell you about her care and comfort.

Tooth-care time

I crunch on dry cat food to keep my teeth and gums in good shape. If you can coax me into it, you can brush my teeth. Be sure to use cat toothpaste and a small, soft brush. Don't use your toothpaste because I'll get sick if I swallow it.

Litter clean-up time

If you clean, empty, and disinfect my litter box often, I'll be content. I like my litter box tucked in a quiet spot — a little privacy, please!

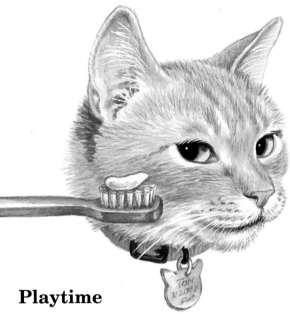

Grooming time

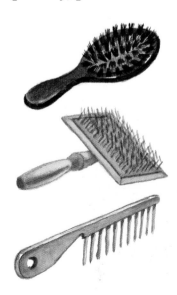

I like to be groomed often. Gently brush me from head to tail and underneath, too. If you run into a tangle, carefully coax it out. And every now and then, I'll need a bath to keep my coat extra clean.

Playtime

Before you and I go outside to play, I need your help. Am I wearing my collar with my rabies tag? And does my ID tag have your name and address on it? The elastic strip on my collar is great. I can free myself more easily if I get caught on a branch.

Nail-care time

Keep a scratching post around so I can stretch up and scrape my claws to clean them. If my nails need clipping, ask an adult to help you. A slip of the clippers can really hurt me.

My cat

☐ loves having her teeth brushed

☐ hates having her teeth brushed

☐ has never had her teeth brushed

When it is fur-brushing time, my cat

☐ runs under the bed

☐ stays still and purrs

☐ or _____

My cat

☐ uses furniture as a scratching post

☐ never scratches furniture

☐ never uses a scratching post

Nap time

Even though I snuggle up in strange places, I like to have my own bed that is my private space. I'm fussy about clean bedding and flea-free sleeping conditions. What about making a one-of-a-kind cat bed for me? It looks great!

Make a one-of-a-kind cat bed

You'll need:

- a cardboard box, big enough for your cat to stretch out in
- scissors
- Magic Markers
- used sheets or towels (make sure no one wants them anymore)

1. Cut away most of one side of the box.
2. Decorate the box with magic markers.
3. Line the box with the sheets or towels.
4. Put the bed in a quiet, cozy corner or in your bedroom. To introduce your cat to her cat bed, gently place her in it and tell her softly you made it for her.

Grooming is gr-r-reat!

When your cat licks his fur from head to tail, he's doing more than keeping his coat spotless. As he grooms, he spreads his fur with his own scent from glands under his skin. If your cat rubs against you, he leaves scent behind to say "I was here." Sometimes your cat grooms to feel relaxed, just as you might feel after a good back rub. If two cats or a mom and kitten groom, they are cleaning each other, sharing their scents, and keeping in touch.

My cat grooming

Waterproofing

As your cat grooms himself, he activates oil glands in his skin. The oil waterproofs his fur and gives him a thin raincoat.

Paw cloth

For those hard-to-reach places such as his head, the back of his neck, and between his shoulders, your cat uses his front paws as wash cloths. He licks his paws and gets to work washing. At the same time, he is spreading his special scent.

Fine-tooth comb

Have you ever tried to comb your hair with your teeth? Your cat combs his fur with his teeth to smooth out tangled, matted hair and remove mud or dirt.

Cooling system

Do you ever splash water on your face when you're hot? Your cat doesn't have to — he has his own clever cooling system. He licks his fur to spread saliva all over himself. As the saliva dries, it evaporates and cools his body.

Tongue twister

What is pink, long, twistable, laps up liquids, can wash a coat, and is rough enough to brush fur? Your cat's amazing tongue!

My cat cleans and grooms when he is feeling

☐ happy

☐ scared

☐ bored

☐ or _____

My cat grooms about _____ times a day.

If I had a tongue like my cat's, I could

_____.

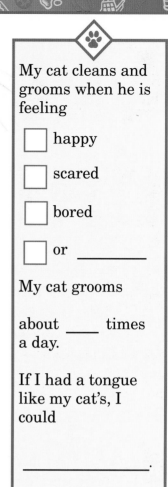

Chill out

Try this cool test to see how your cat's cooling system works.

1. Moisten a spot on the inside of your wrist with a dot of warm water.

2. Blow gently on the wet spot, then blow on a nearby dry area on the same wrist. Which spot feels cooler?

Most people find the wet spot feels cooler. When you blow, your warm breath propels some of the water from the wet spot on your wrist into the air. This process, called evaporation, takes heat away from your body with the water, and the spot feels cool. Your cat's saliva evaporates from his fur and leaves his body feeling cooler.

What's for dinner?

It's dinnertime and you dish out the same cat food again. Boring, you think, but your cat might tell you differently. A balanced diet of nutritious cat food keeps her active and healthy.

And a steady diet of the same kind of food prevents stomach upsets due to diet changes. So bring on the familiar cat food! What better dinner could you serve your special friend?

What should I feed my cat?

You have a choice of dry, semi-moist, or canned cat food, but most vets suggest you serve dry food. It is very nutritious and when your cat crunches and munches it, she keeps her teeth and gums in good shape. If you want to add a little canned food, that's fine but not necessary. When you choose a brand of cat food, be sure the label says "low ash" and "balanced diet."

What about feeding my cat fish and meat?

If your cat gets a balanced diet in her cat food, she doesn't need extra tidbits of cooked fish and meat. There might be bacteria in raw meat and fish and your cat could get sick. So don't take a chance: leave them off the menu. And keep all bones out of her reach. Bones can splinter and injure your cat's body inside.

Can my cat have table scraps?

Every now and then you can give your cat a tiny treat. Too many extras fill her stomach with food that isn't as healthy for her as her own cat food.

What should my cat drink?

Milk often upsets cats' stomachs. Give your cat fresh water each day in a clean bowl and she'll be content.

When should I feed my cat?

Set out a certain amount of food at the same time each day and let your cat snack when she pleases. Give your cat her own dish — although if you have more than one cat, they may prefer to share! Be sure to always place your cat's dish in the same spot. A familiar routine will make her happy.

How much should I feed my cat?

Your cat can easily become overweight, so don't stuff her with more than she needs. Kittens usually require several small meals a day, and adults thrive on one or two a day.

In one day, my cat nibbles a bowl of food as big as

☐ a Ping-Pong ball

☐ a baseball

☐ or _____

_____

My cat takes ____ laps of water at one time.

If my cat made her own dinner, she would make

_____.

Cat treats

Make delicious cat treats for special days. Give them out just a nibble at a time, since new foods can upset your cat's stomach.

You'll need:

- 1/2 cup (125 ml) canned sardines, drained
- 1 cup (250 ml) whole-wheat bread crumbs
- 1 tablespoon (15 ml) vegetable oil
- 1 egg, beaten
- fork, big bowl, small spoon, cookie sheet, sealed storage jar

Be sure to ask for an adult's permission before using the oven.

1. Preheat the oven to 325°F (160°C).
2. Using the fork, mash the sardines in the bowl.
3. Mix in the bread crumbs, oil, and egg.
4. Drop the batter from the small spoon onto the cookie sheet and bake for 10 minutes.
5. Cool and save in a sealed jar in the refrigerator.

Cat talk

When your cat rubs against you or looks at you wide-eyed and worried, he doesn't need to make a sound. His whole body talks for him, especially his face, eyes, ears, whiskers, and tail. Look at some of the things these cats are saying. Does your cat talk in these ways?

Fill in the blanks or check off the boxes that best describe your cat.

Contented cat

Does your cat loll on his back, relaxed and purring with his eyes half shut? This is the sign of a secure, happy cat.

When my cat feels happy, he

☐ likes to loll on his back

☐ doesn't like to loll on his back

When my cat feels happy, he also

_____.

Scaredy-cat

Even though your cat feels fearful, he might try to fool his enemy. He makes his hair stand up and arches his back. With his tail held high, he looks one size larger. But his tipped-back ears and wide-open pupils give him away. He's really a scaredy-cat!

Yikes! When my cat is afraid, his whiskers

☐ point back

☐ stick out to the side

☐ fan forward

When my cat is frightened, he also

_____.

We're friends

As your cat brushes his head and body against you, he is saying, "We're friends" and "I like to be close to you." At the same time he leaves his unique scent from glands on his mouth, head and tail. That's his special marker. And he takes in your smell, too.

My cat likes to rub against me when

- [ ] I first come home
- [ ] he thinks I am leaving
- [ ] or _____

_____.

Cat chatter

"Meow" can mean "I'm hungry!," "Don't leave me!," or "Get out of bed!" Even though meows mean many different things, they are not the only sounds that cats make. Some people can tell the difference among as many as 16 different cat sounds. And cats probably communicate with each other using many more sounds. Certain breeds are more "talkative" than others. Do you have a very "chatty" cat?

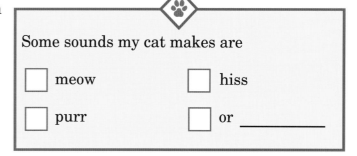

Some sounds my cat makes are

- [ ] meow
- [ ] hiss
- [ ] purr
- [ ] or _____

Look out!

Your cat gives clear signs when he is angry or about to attack. Look out and stay away! If you see his ears back, his mouth open to hiss or spit, his lips curled back to show sharp teeth, your cat is ready for action.

My cat

- [ ] likes to fight
- [ ] doesn't like to fight

When my cat looks angry, I

_____

_____

_____.

Paw prints

Does your cat race out the door in sneakers, tug on warm boots for the cold, or snuggle up at night wearing slippers? No! She's lucky — her paws are her sneakers, boots, and slippers all in one! She also uses her paws for pouncing, climbing, and to defend herself. Trace your cat's paw in the picture frame below. Then gently examine the pads and claws on her paw and draw them in.

My cat's paw print

Climbing gear

As fast as lightning, a cat can scoot up a tree. She clings with her climbing gear: her needle-sharp claws. Look carefully at your cat's paws to see where she hides her claws. She pulls them into tiny pockets in her paws where they stay sharp and safe until she needs them.

Sneakers

Protective pads on her paws cushion your cat's body when she lands from a jump. If she tucks in her claws, she can silently creep up on you with her soft, padded sneakers. She's just practicing for the hunt.

Cool cat

Your cat's soft paw pads are also cooling devices. When she's hot, she sweats through her paw pads. The sweat moistens the pads to keep them soft and free from cracks. If she has been perspiring a lot, she will leave a trail of sweaty paw prints behind.

Socks and slippers

Warm fur on your cat's paws and between her toes are her socks and slippers. It's easy for her to stay comfortable and cozy.

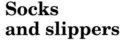

When my cat creeps up on me

☐ I always know my cat is there

☐ I jump because my cat startles me

☐ or _____

_____

My cat has _____ toes on each front paw and ___ toes on each back paw.

Make a paw print

Make a print of your cat's paw to show your friends or hang on a wall. You will need your cat's help, so be sure to find a time when she feels content and cooperative.

You'll need:

- 1/2 cup (125 ml) flour
- 1/2 cup (125 ml) cornmeal
- 1/2 cup (125 ml) water
- large spoon, big bowl, old plastic plate that is no longer needed, water-based paints (optional), stick-on picture hanger (optional)

1. Mix the flour and cornmeal in the bowl.
2. Add the water slowly while stirring the mixture.
3. Put some of the mixture onto the plate.
4. Wet your cat's paw well and press it gently into the plate to make an imprint.
5. Let the imprint dry completely — it may take up to a week.
6. Decorate with paints, if you like.
7. If you want to hang the print on the wall, attach the picture hanger to the back of the plate.

Super senses

I f you and your cat played a game to see who had the keenest sense of smell, touch, taste, hearing, or sight, your cat would win hands down!

These sharp senses are necessary in the wild for cats to sneak up and catch their prey. Your cat has the same amazing senses. Watch and you will see them at work!

Pre-taste test

Cats are usually fussy eaters, but that's a good thing. They smell their food to test it before they taste it. If the food is going bad, cats are very sensitive to the odors caused by chemical changes in it. They wisely turn away if their food is not the very best!

Nimble tumble

Did you know that your cat's ears are used for more than hearing? When a cat tumbles from a tree, messages from his inner ears to his brain help him gain his balance and prepare him for landing. As he falls, he flips his flexible body over and usually lands on his feet, which saves his head and back from injury. When he touches down, he arches his back to cushion the impact. Unlike other animals, cats can survive some amazing falls. But some tumbles do injure cats, so be sure to keep yours away from very high places.

Super sniffer

Your cat's nose gives him all sorts of news. He smells scents left by other cats and knows they have passed by. He smells his own scent that he has rubbed on things and feels secure knowing he is home. He smells when you are home. Your cat's nose looks little, but the smelling area inside is much bigger than yours. That's what gives him his superior sniffer.

Nose print

Did you know that your cat's nose covering is different from any other cat's? His nose print is unique, just as your fingerprint is.

Home sweet home

Have you heard stories of courageous cats finding their way home from far away? It does happen, but nobody really knows how. Some people say cats use their sensitive senses, and others say there is more to it.

Extra sense

No wonder your cat has excellent senses! He has an extra sense that combines taste and smell. This special sense is usually used by the male to find a mate.

Is there a mouse in the house?

Your cat will hear if there is a mouse around, but you won't hear the squeak. That's because your cat hears much higher-pitched sounds than you do or even dogs do. When your cat hears an "eek, eek," he looks alert and rotates his cup-shaped ears toward the noise. Cup your hands behind your ears as someone speaks to you. Is the sound any clearer?

Catnip whiff-and-sniff toy

Make a catnip toy for your cat to play with. Catnip is a plant that most cats love to sniff. You can grow it in your garden or buy it dried.

You'll need:

- used tissue paper
- dried catnip
- a sturdy piece of cloth cut about half the size of this page
- a piece of string about as long as your arm

1. Scrunch the tissue paper into a ball.

2. Place the tissue paper ball and some catnip in the middle of the cloth.

3. Gather up the sides to make a ball. Ask an adult to help you tie the bundle securely with string.

4. When your cat is feeling playful, give him this whiff-and-sniff toy. If catnip doesn't excite your cat, give him the toy just to bat around.

Note: do not give catnip to kittens under six months of age.

When my cat is around catnip he
☐ rolls over and over
☐ jumps in the air
☐ does a dance
☐ ignores it

Eye spy

On a dark night sprinkled with stars, your cat creeps out. Pounce! As quick as a wink, a mouse is in her mouth. Your cat is using all her keen senses, particularly her hearing and sight. Because of your cat's amazing night sight, her eyes spy tiny moving creatures that you couldn't see at all.

Night sight

Cats can't see when it is totally black. But their vision is six times better than ours in very low light. That's because of a mirror-like layer that cats have at the back of their eyes. This layer reflects light, no matter how faint, inside cats' eyes and so increases the effect of the light. These reflecting "mirrors" also give the glow to your cat's night eyes.

On-target vision

Cats have excellent vision for hunting. Like the eyes of most animals that hunt, your cat's eyes are on the front of her face so they work together to snap an extremely accurate picture of an object even if it is far away.

My cat's eyes

Safety glasses

When your cat is resting, she covers her eyes with her extra eyelids that are somewhat see-through. Now her eyes are protected from dust and she can still keep an eye on you!

My cat has eyes as big as _____

_____ .

My cat's eyes look like _____
in the dark.

Open me, close me

Open a window shade and light comes in, close the shade and light stays out. Your cat's pupil, the dark center of her eye, works in a similar way. The pupils open extra wide to let light in at night and close to tiny slits to keep light out in bright daylight.

Cat's eye test

Try this eye test to find out more about your cat's eyes.

1. Carefully observe the pupils (the dark part) in your cat's eyes throughout a day.
2. Beside each time shown below, fill in what the pupils look like at that time. Are they large and round or are they tiny slits?
3. A few days later, watch your cat's pupils and see if they are open or closed at the same times of the day.

Here are my cat's eyes:

morning

noon

night

On the move

D o a cat stretch. Now pounce like a cat. Try walking along a narrow board, close to the ground, without falling off. It's easy if you're a cat. Cats are amazing gymnasts. They have great agility, accuracy, and grace. Their bodies are supremely suited for stealth and instant action in the hunt. Take a look at the cat skeleton below and you'll see how your cat is shaped to be on the move.

Tail

When you walk along a narrow board, you stick out your arms sideways to balance your body. Your cat's tail is his balance pole. It helps him balance on a fence when he strolls along, turns, or jumps off.

Spine and neck bones

Your cat can reach almost anywhere on his body when he grooms. The bones of his long, supple spine and neck have muscular connections between them that give his body amazing flexibility.

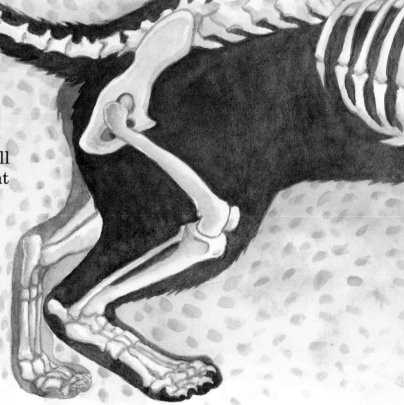

Knees

The knees take some of the stress when your cat lands from running or jumping. Inside the knee are small "shock absorbers." Did you know that your knees work in much the same way as your cat's?

Back leg bones

Watch your cat push off to jump or run. He uses his powerful back legs for takeoff. Large leg muscles attached to the bones provide strength and spring. Look how long and sturdy these bones are. A cat can jump about five times his own length.

Shoulder bones

When you try to squeeze through a small space, it's not your head that stops you, it's your wide shoulders. Your cat's shoulder bones are narrow and placed flat against the side of his chest. This allows him to fit through tiny places. His shoulder bones also keep his front legs close together, making it easy for him to put one paw in front of the other and walk along a narrow board.

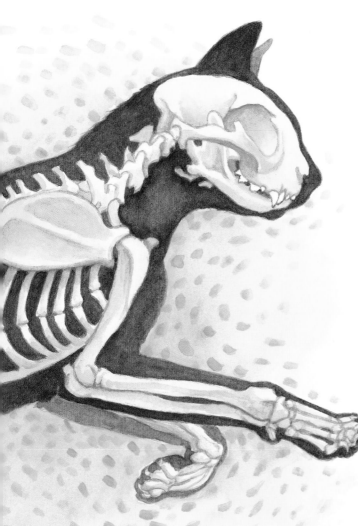

Toes

Your cat's foot is shaped so that he walks and runs on his tiptoes. This way, he moves lightly, quickly, and quietly. Try running on your tiptoes. How does it feel?

Crazy cork

Make this easy toy for your cat, then watch the amazing moves he makes.

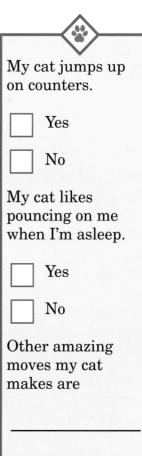

You'll need:

- a piece of string that measures from about your shoulder to the floor
- a cork

1. Securely tie the string around the cork (ask an adult to help you, if you like) and hang it from a doorknob so that it's low enough for your cat to reach.

2. Draw your cat's attention to the cork, and then the fun begins!

Shoulder joints

Your cat's flexible shoulder joints give him freedom to turn his front legs in different directions. Just watch him wash and groom!

My cat jumps up on counters.

☐ Yes

☐ No

My cat likes pouncing on me when I'm asleep.

☐ Yes

☐ No

Other amazing moves my cat makes are

_____

_____ .

Vet visit

Your cat won't remind you when it's time for a visit to the veterinarian. Ask an adult to check the calendar, telephone for an appointment, and take you along with your cat. Save up all your questions about your cat and take them along, too. Here are some you might have wondered about.

Why does my cat's fur fall out when she comes for her checkup?

Your cat feels nervous in a new place. Tiny nerve endings by the base of each hair get the message and activate the hair to fall out. The soft fur seems to fly everywhere!

Why does my cat purr?

It's a mystery! Cats purr when they are content, but they also purr when they feel anxious. Nobody knows why.

Will my cat have kittens?

Your cat will probably parent kittens unless you have your cat neutered. Decide with your parents if you want to look after more cats. If your special pet is enough for you to care for, take your cat to the vet's for a neutering operation. Kittens are adorable, but there are thousands born each year that are not wanted.

Does my cat need to have shots?

Yes, your cat has to have her shots to keep her free from cat diseases. Kittens should receive a series of shots from the time they are six weeks old to the time they are four months old. Adult cats require shots once a year.

If my cat scratches, does she have fleas?

If fleas have set up house in your cat's furry coat, you and your cat might not even know it. Only cats who are allergic to fleas will itch and scratch. And some cats itch because of other allergies, parasites, or dry, infected skin. Check your cat's coat often. Fleas are there if you see what look like bits of black pepper. Ask your vet what to use for the unwanted guests.

How do I know if my cat is sick?

If you don't feel like playing or eating and are tired and droopy, you know you are sick. Your cat feels the same way when she is ill. Here are some signs of sickness to look for:

- no appetite
- more thirsty than usual
- runny eyes or nose
- dull coat and doesn't groom
- diarrhea
- vomiting
- breathing difficulties
- unusual behavior such as hiding from you

If your cat shows any of these signs, ask an adult to call your veterinarian.

Can I take my cat outside?

Cats are well suited for indoor living. It protects them from fleas, cat fights, and car accidents. You can introduce your cat to the outdoors if you like, but be careful at first. Put your cat in a harness attached to a rope. Let her explore a little each day with the harness on, then gradually allow her to roam without the harness for short periods of time.

How do I know if my cat is healthy?

Your pet is in the best of health when she has shiny eyes, a glossy coat, is active, alert, and eats well. After she grooms her coat with pride, give her a hug and you'll have a happy cat as well as a healthy one!

My cat ☐ is afraid of new places

☐ likes to explore new places

When my cat was at the vet's, my cat

_____.

How can I prepare my cat for a visit to the vet?

A week or two before your cat's appointment, put her carrying case in a room she plays in. Leave it open and put two Ping-Pong balls inside. When your cat starts to play with the balls, roll them back inside for her to find. Make the game fun so she will go in and out of the carrying case and be comfortable with it. Put her gently inside and take her on small outings around the block. When it's time for a vet visit, she won't mind her carrier.

Travel tips

Hooray! It's vacation time! You've been telling your cat about this special trip for weeks. As you stuff things into your backpack, you glance down to see an anxious, furry face. Pick up your cat and tell him he is really coming with you. Then snuggle up with him and make a cat checklist together.

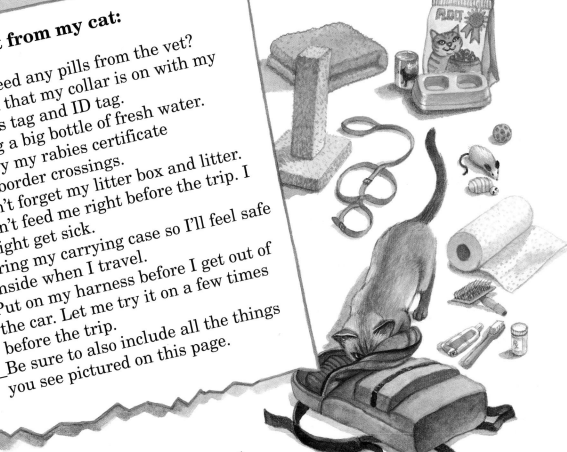

Checklist from my cat:

___Do I need any pills from the vet?

___Check that my collar is on with my rabies tag and ID tag.

___Bring a big bottle of fresh water.

___Carry my rabies certificate for border crossings.

___Don't forget my litter box and litter.

___Don't feed me right before the trip. I might get sick.

___Bring my carrying case so I'll feel safe inside when I travel.

___Put on my harness before I get out of the car. Let me try it on a few times before the trip.

___Be sure to also include all the things you see pictured on this page.

Trips my cat and I have been on are

☐ to my grandparents' house

☐ to a foreign country

☐ or _____

If my cat and I could go anywhere, we would go to

_____

_____ .

Pet papers

Here is a special pocket to hold some very important things for your cat.

In this pocket are:

☐ Cat papers

☐ Vet papers

☐ Vaccination records

☐ Extra photos

☐ Keepsakes

☐ Other _____

_____

Vet's phone number

_____

Cat license or ID tag number

_____

Ask an adult to photocopy the papers you want to keep and slip your set inside here.

How to make a pocket to keep all your cat's records and treasures.

1. Fold the page along the dotted line as shown.

2. Attach this page to the back cover by taping along the top and bottom edges.

Acknowledgements

A special thank-you to Dr. Greg Usher for his expertise and generous assistance.

An appreciative thank-you to the following people: Brenda Clark for her lively illustrations; Overdrive for its creative design; my editor, Liz MacLeod, for her humor and unerring eye; and to everyone at Kids Can Press.

A warm thank-you to my friends who took the time to tell me all about their pets, and a hug for Charlie who is always there to encourage me.

Consultant: Dr. Greg Usher, Rosedale Animal Hospital, Toronto, Ontario

Text copyright © 1994 by Marilyn Baillie
Illustrations copyright © 1994 by Brenda Clark

First U.S. Edition
Published in Canada by Kids Can Press Ltd.

ISBN 0-316-07688-0
Library of Congress Catalog Card Number 93-86659

10 9 8 7 6 5 4 3 2 1

Printed in Hong Kong